I Want a Cuddle!

For Neil and for Lizzie who gave me the idea
MB

For my family
JP

ISBN 0-439-66788-7

Text copyright © 2001 by Malorie Blackman. Illustrations copyright © 2001 by Joanne Partis.
All rights reserved. Published by Orchard Books, an imprint of Scholastic Inc.
ORCHARD BOOKS and design are registered trademarks of Watts Publishing Group, Ltd.,
used under license. SCHOLASTIC and associated logos are trademarks and/or
registered trademarks of Scholastic Inc.

12 11 10 9 8 7 6 5 4 3   11 12 13 14 15/0

Printed in the U.S.A.   40

First Scholastic paperback printing, April 2004

I Want a Cuddle!

Malorie Blackman
Illustrated by Joanne Partis

SCHOLASTIC INC.

New York Toronto London Auckland Sydney
Mexico City New Delhi Hong Kong Buenos Aires

Little Rabbit and her friends
were playing peek-a-boo, when. . .

BUMP! THUMP!
Poor Little Rabbit!

"What's the matter, Little Rabbit?"
asked Hedgehog.
"I've hurt my paw and I want a
cuddle," sobbed Little Rabbit.
"I'll cuddle you," said Hedgehog.

"Ooh," said Little Rabbit. "You're too prickly." So off she hopped. . .

"Why are you crying, Little Rabbit?" asked Squirrel.
"I've hurt my paw and I want a cuddle,"
sniffed Little Rabbit.

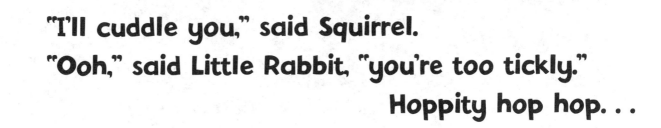

"I'll cuddle you," said Squirrel.
"Ooh," said Little Rabbit, "you're too tickly."
Hoppity hop hop. . .

"Why are you so sad, Little Rabbit?"
asked Badger.
  "I've hurt my paw and I want
a cuddle," said Little Rabbit.
  "I'll cuddle you," said Badger.
  "Ooh," said Little Rabbit,
"you're far too bristly."
        Hoppity hop hop...

"Hey! What's wrong, Little Rabbit?" asked Toad.
"I've hurt my paw and I want a cuddle,"
said Little Rabbit.
"I'll cuddle you," said Toad.

"Ooh," said Little Rabbit, "you're far too lumpy. And the parts that aren't lumpy are squidgy and bumpy! I want my mom."

And Little Rabbit set off
home through the forest.

Little Rabbit was
so busy hopping
along. . .

that she didn't see who
was creeping and
sneaking up behind her. . .

Little Fox!

"What are you doing, Little Rabbit?" asked Little Fox, licking his lips.

"I fell over and hurt my paw," said Little Rabbit, "and now I'm going home for a cuddle."

And off Little Rabbit hopped. . .

"I'll **CUDDLE** you," said Little Fox.

OOOMPHS!

"No, thank you," replied Little Rabbit.

Hop! Jump!

"I'll **HUG** you then!" said Little Fox.

RAAGH!

"No, thanks," called out Little Rabbit.
Hop! Jump! Skip!

"I'll give you a **BIG SQUEEZE** then!"

EEEEEEE EEK!

"I don't think so," said
Little Rabbit.
Hop! Jump! Skip! Leap!

"I'll **EAT YOU** then!" And Little Fox pounced at Little Rabbit.

But he missed.

Little Fox sat down,
opened his mouth and
HOWLED! "I want a cuddle.

I want a **CUDDLE**."

Little Rabbit stopped.
Poor Little Fox!
Little Rabbit went over to
him, opened her paws and. . .

gave Little Fox a great
big cuddle!

"I'm going home to my mom,"
sniffed Little Fox.

"So am I," said Little Rabbit.

"Thanks for the cuddle,"
said Little Fox.

"You're welcome,"
said Little Rabbit.

And hop! hop! went Little
Rabbit all the way home.

"Mom, Mom, I hurt my paw and Little Fox chased after me. I want a cuddle! Where's my cuddle?"

"Right here," said Mother Rabbit. And she cuddled Little Rabbit tight, tight, tight.

"Oh, Mom!" said Little Rabbit. "Your cuddle feels just right!"